F IS FOR FREEDOM

BY RONI SCHOTTER

ILLUSTRATED BY

C. B. MORDAN

DORLING KINDERSLEY PUBLISHING, INC.

ACKNOWLEDGMENTS

The author gratefully acknowledges the help of the following people and organizations: Dorothy Carter; Jane Weiss; Diana Engel; Amanda Dargan; Steve Zeitlin; William P. Kelly; Kathy Browning, Tenant House Coordinator, Philipsburg Manor, Historic Hudson Valley; Steve Kozak, Farm Manager, Philipsburg Manor, Historic Hudson Valley; Dina Rose Friedman, Site Director, Sunnyside, Historic Hudson Valley; Stephanie Hall, Archive of Folk Music, Library of Congress; Judith Gray, Head of Reference, American Folklife Center, Library of Congress; Hastings Historical Society; Susan Feir, Hastings-on-Hudson Public Library; Rinker Buck; Roger Panetta; Ross Higgins, Director of Programs, Historic Hudson Valley; Jerry Silverman; and, especially, Melanie Kroupa.

A Melanie Kroupa Book

Dorling Kindersley Publishing, Inc.
95 Madison Avenue
New York, New York 10016

Visit us on the World Wide Web at http://www.dk.com

Library of Congress Cataloging-in-Publication Data

Schotter, Roni.
F Is for Freedom / by Roni Schotter.—1st ed.
p. cm.
"A DK Ink book."
Summary: When ten-year-old Manda interrupts a midnight delivery, she discovers her parents' involvement in the Underground Railroad and makes her own contributions to a fugitive slave's freedom.
ISBN 0-7894-2641-2
1. Underground railroad—Juvenile fiction. [1. Underground railroad—Fiction. 2. Fugitive slaves—Fiction. 3. Slavery—Fiction. 4. Afro-Americans—Fiction. 5. Friendship–Fiction.] I. Title

PZ7.S3765 Fae 2000
[Fic]—dc21 99-462048

Book design by Sylvia Frezzolini Severance
The illustrations for this book were prepared using scratchboard.
The text of this book is set in 12.5-point New Baskerville.
Hand lettering on page 95 by Mary Buonocore
Printed and bound in U.S.A.

First Edition, 2000
2 4 6 8 10 9 7 5 3 1

For Richard and Jesse

The alphabet is an abolitionist.

If you would keep the people enslaved,
refuse to teach them to read.

—Harper's Weekly, *1867*

Knowledge unfits a child to be a slave.

—Frederick Douglass

One

A noise . . . In the dark of her room, in bed, Amanda listened. A rustling. One sharp knock, then a double thump. *Ghosts?* No, only the wind in its autumn hurry, rushing through trees outside, rattling bone-dry leaves and carelessly knocking and spilling hard brown acorns on the slate roof.

Amanda glanced nervously about and clutched her doll Coey Yocks. At the foot of her bed lay the book with the wonderfully frightening story in it, the one she'd been reading just before she blew her candle out, when she was supposed to have gone to sleep. Instead, Amanda had been playacting the way she did almost every night, using Coey Yocks to pretend the scary story in her book. There was absolutely nothing to fear. Only her imagination.

But then . . . a cry like a cat, the high whinny of horses, and strange voices behind the house. The headless horseman? Trembling, Amanda grabbed her candle and Coey Yocks for comfort. Tiptoeing past her brother Thomas, still asleep in his small bed, she crept quietly downstairs and into the night.

Outside, the world blinked bright, then dark again, as night clouds played hide-and-seek with the moon.

Shadow shapes appeared and disappeared on the lawn. Hidden behind a bush, Amanda watched as her father and a mysterious man unloaded a wagon piled high with barrels and sacks. Near them stood her mother, whispering, looking worried.

Was Amanda dreaming? Two of the sacks stood up and began to move and shake in the flickering moonlight. They *were* ghosts, and they were . . . dancing! "Mama!" Amanda cried out, and ran to her.

"Manda!" her mother cried. "You should be in bed!"

"Hush!" Her father whispered a warning as a dark face, a matching neck, and a pair of grain-speckled shoulders emerged from one of the sacks.

Amanda started to scream again, but her mother's hand covered her mouth. "You've seen nothing, nor heard anything," she said. Manda nodded, clutching Coey Yocks to her chest. Drawing the skirt of her mother's robe around her, she peered out.

A woman with skin the color of Mama's molasses stepped out of the grain sack holding a small brown baby asleep in her arms. She smiled shyly at Amanda's father, who nodded silently and then helped open the smaller sack.

Out sprang a tall, thin girl around Manda's age, who ran to the woman and hugged her. And then, out of a barrel, a man, long and dark, like a licorice stick, twisted his way out, bits of oat caught in the curls of his hair. He clasped the stranger's hand, then her father's. "My family, we much obliged," he said quietly.

"Our privilege," the stranger whispered.

"Hurry" was Amanda's father's only reply. Where had

Papa's manners gone, Manda wondered? This wasn't like him. And who was this family that had come with the night? Where were they from? Why were they here? Amanda's busy mind was abuzz with questions. No chance to figure answers, for her mother had taken Amanda's hand and was pulling her toward Papa.

"You'd best be on your way," Papa whispered to the man who had brought the family in his wagon.

"You're right, friend," the man agreed. "Just as soon as I've set things straight on my wagon, I'll be leaving."

"It's good work you've done today," Papa said, shaking the man's hand.

"And good work you'll be doing. Now you best be doing it."

"True enough," Papa said, and motioned to Mama. Holding tightly to her mother's hand, Amanda followed Papa as he led them, and the mysterious family, into their house.

Two

Down the side hallway behind Papa they filed. The only sound was the creak and crunch of footsteps on floorboards—some with shoes and, Amanda noticed, staring at the tall man's earth-encrusted feet, some without. Closer and closer they came to the big closet at the end of the hall, the one her father had told Amanda never, under any circumstances, to open.

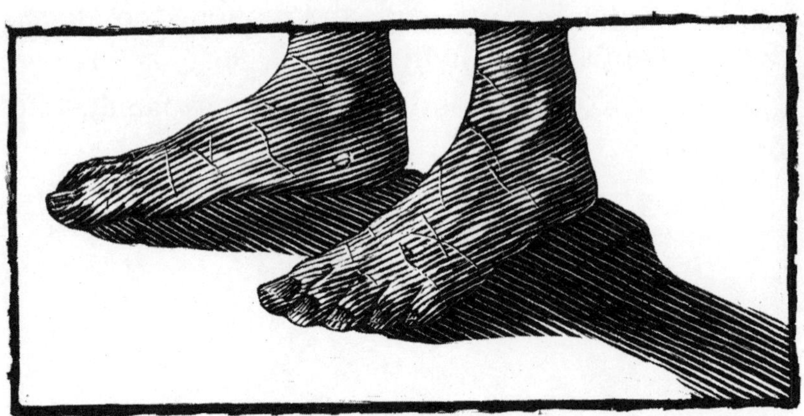

Amanda held her breath as her father took a key out of his pocket and unlocked the forbidden door. To Amanda's surprise, there was nothing inside but rope and some old clothing. Shoving it aside, her father began to knock on the wall at the back of the closet. *Tap-tap,* he knocked. *Rap-rap.* The wall began to shudder. Then, with a squeal, it parted and . . . opened!

"Inside," Papa said to the strangers.

Inside? Why would Papa . . . ?

"Inside *now,*" Papa called out sharply, as the sound of horses' hooves rang out on the road. What other visitors could possibly be arriving so late at night, Amanda wondered.

"Isaac!" the dark woman whispered fearfully to her husband. The baby began to whimper, and as the whimper changed to a high, catlike cry, Amanda recognized it as the sound she had heard earlier.

"No noise!" Amanda's father commanded, but he needn't have, for the baby's mother had already opened a glass vial and was dripping some amber-colored drops down the baby's throat.

A second later, the crying ceased. The mother covered the baby's tiny mouth with her hand, exactly the way Amanda's mother had done with hers, and swiftly the baby fell back to sleep.

"Hurry," Amanda's father whispered for the second time that night. The frightened family obeyed, climbing quickly through the closet opening and disappearing into the darkness beyond. Papa pulled the closet wall shut, pushed the rope and the clothing back in place, and locked the door, just as someone began to knock loudly out front. "Come along," he urged Amanda and her mother. His face had lost its usual color. It was hard and tight as a turnip.

"Manda," he whispered, kneeling down till he was eye-to-eye with her. "You are always using your imagination and playacting. You know I don't usually encourage you, but now . . . now is a time to see how good you are at it. Only remember what Mama told you: You've seen nothing here tonight, nor heard anything."

Amanda nodded, too scared and far too confused to speak. She wanted to do as her papa asked. She tried to blot out the sight of the strange family stuffed into the dreadful, dark closet. She tried to blot out the sound of their voices and of the baby's cry. It wasn't possible. Her heart beat as loudly as the knocker on the front door. What did her father mean about using her imagination and playacting? She had no time to ask, for her mother was already opening the door.

There, standing before them, with his dreadful snake eyes, was the county constable, Charlie Meecker. He was chewing, as always, on a piece of dried meat. With him was his deputy, One-Word Jake. "Suspicious!" was all Jake said.

Three

"Mrs. Van Dorn," Mr. Meecker said, tucking a wad of meat into the pocket of his cheek with his tongue and bowing politely to Amanda's mother. "John," he said, with anger. "Something foul's afoot. Now, don't try to deny it. There's a man outside claims he's making a delivery. At this hour! And Jake and me, we heard a baby cry. You wouldn't be hiding runaways, would you, John? Someone with your sympathies. You wouldn't be hiding colored folk? You know the penalties for that."

Amanda's heart stopped. Runaways! Escaped slaves! So that's what they were. She'd heard rumor of them hiding in the woods on their way to Canada and freedom, but it had all seemed like a story in one of the books her uncle Oliver had given her. Something strange and faraway and certainly not real.

"Now calm down, Charlie," Amanda heard her father say, and she felt her heart begin to beat again. "Didn't know you had such an imagination! Why, that's Bill Turner out there, from down in Jersey. Y'ever hear of mud? Got stuck in some on the way here, halfway up the wheels of his wagon. Why, I've been expecting him since noon, and he only just arrived. He and I, we traded. I gave him a load of my hay, some apples, a few chickens, and one of my best laying hens for his grain. Got scarcely enough feed for the animals this winter coming, so I figured I'd best be bartering me some."

"That's a mighty nice story, John," Mr. Meecker said, staring at Papa through his narrow snake eyes and chewing ever so slowly on the wad of meat in his cheek. "Jake, maybe you better go outside and take a look at those wheels. Sure hope they're caked with mud, for your sake, John. But tell me, what about that crying we heard?"

"Oh, that," Amanda's mother answered quickly, nervously. "That was . . . poor Amanda. The noise of the delivery woke her. Then she couldn't find her little doll, Curly Locks. Even though she's half grown, she never goes anywhere without it. Keeps it for comfort. She calls it Coey Yocks 'cause when she was a little one she couldn't say her *L*'s. Tell Mr. Meecker about it, Manda. Tell him how . . . how you lost your doll."

Amanda was amazed. Her mother, who always told the truth, was lying and asking her to do the same! All of a sudden Amanda understood what her papa had meant. It was time to use her imagination and begin her playacting. This was Mama giving her her cue.

Four

Amanda closed her eyes, trying to imagine how she would feel if she really lost Coey Yocks. That was easy. It would be terrible. Coey Yocks was part of her. Same as her heart and her hand were. She'd had Coey Yocks since forever, since the moment her mother first made her—stitching bits of rag together for a body, then stuffing the rag with fluffy cotton, sewing a button on for a nose, embroidering blue cross-stitches for eyes, red line backstitch for lips, and attaching curly yellow wool for hair, then presenting it to Amanda along with a kiss. Amanda knew she was a bit too grown-up to care so much for a doll, but she couldn't help it. She intended to keep Coey Yocks forever. Amanda opened her eyes and looked straight at Mr. Meecker.

"I . . . I . . . woke up. I . . . couldn't find Coey Yocks and I started to cry," she stammered, and to her surprise, tears welled in her eyes and spilled down her cheeks. She was imagining it all so perfectly. She could see it. The picture she was creating in her imagination, along with the fear and excitement of the night and the terrible lie she was telling Mr. Meecker—a grown-up and the county constable besides—well, she was crying now and it wasn't an act.

Mr. Meecker's narrowed eyes were upon her.

"I didn't mean to cry," Amanda said, pushing her

imagination even further. "I was frightened by the noise outside, so I woke up and got out of bed." (Well, at least that was true!) "And then I couldn't find Coey Yocks. I searched and searched and finally I found her . . . under my bed." (A second lie. This one was easier than the last! It was just as her mama and papa had always told her. Once a person started lying, new lies sprouted faster than weeds did in a garden.) "I'm sorry I caused such trouble!" Amanda wailed, starting to enjoy herself. She forced her voice higher and higher till it sounded like a baby's shrieking cry. "And I'm sorry I caused you to come in the night, Mr. Meecker. Oh, Papa! Oh, Mama! Can you ever forgive me?"

With the last question, Amanda surprised even herself. She let out a wondrous wail, opening her mouth wider and wider, marveling at the sound she was able to

produce. With little effort, the wail soared on high, bumped, then shattered against the ceiling, turning into a perfect scream. Not bad, Amanda thought, impressed with her talent. She filled her lungs and clasped her hands together, as if fervently praying for forgiveness, all the while maintaining the piercing and perfect scream.

As for Charlie Meecker's hands, they, too, were clasped, but *his* were over his ears. "Hush that child, Amelia!" he pleaded. "Hush her! *Please!*"

"Well, now, she's upset, Mr. Meecker," Mama said nervously, eyeing Amanda. "You know how it is with some children."

"That's enough, Amanda!" her papa said, and when Amanda looked up at him, she saw that he meant it.

Manda sniffed a few times, dabbed at her eyes, and looked plaintively up at Charlie Meecker. She was kind of sorry Papa had said, "That's enough." She had just imagined something wonderfully exciting and slightly dangerous to do next, a thing she'd read about but never seen. She had planned to faint right at Mr. Meecker's feet—a careful faint, one just shy of his disgustingly dirty boots. Now *that* would have done it!

One-Word Jake came in from outside. "Mud" was all he said.

"Mud," Mr. Meecker sighed. He took a couple of slow chews on the mass of meat in his mouth, then swallowed. "Looks like you win, John. But just the same, Jake and me will have to have a look about. There's a Franklin Williams, owns one of them big plantations down in the Carolinas, put out this handbill. Seems he's lost some property. A whole family of slaves. Rumor is they've made it up North, maybe to this area."

"So, leave them, Charlie," Papa said. "They're free once they're north of the Mason-Dixon line."

"Not anymore, John. You know the new slave law. Used to be I could look the other way. Can't anymore. Like it or not, I have a new job now: Catch any runaways and send 'em back down South to their owners. There's a price on their heads and a prison sentence of six months for anyone trying to help or hide 'em. That, and a thousand-dollar fine! Be careful, John. You and your sympathies could get you into trouble. Read this while Jake and me take our look. Maybe it'll keep you from doing something foolish."

He put a handbill in Papa's hand. Then he and Jake set off down the long side hallway—straight toward the closet.

Five

"John!" Amanda's mother whispered. "What shall we do?"

"If I knew, I would be doing it. Nothing left but to hope and pray they find nothing."

Mr. Meecker and One-Word Jake were out of sight now, in the kitchen, poking around among the pots and pans and making a terrible clatter. Did they think they'd find someone hidden under the kettle or the colander?

"Manda," her papa said, bending to whisper in her ear, "you did a fine job with your playacting, even if you did get a bit carried away. It's a piece of luck that your brother Thomas is such a sound sleeper and wasn't awakened by your histrionics! I hope you know that you shouldn't ever say what is untrue. Only now, because we . . . " Her papa's voice trailed off. His eyes had fallen on the handbill and its large black letters. He stood up.

"What do you think, Amelia?" Papa whispered. "I thought to keep all this from her, but she knows nearly everything now. Might as well let her read the rest." Manda's mother sighed and nodded.

Proud to be considered a grown-up and prouder still that she was as good as any grown-up at reading, Amanda read the paper in Papa's hand:

LOST PROPERTY

RUN AWAY FROM SUBSCRIBER, on Thursday, the 2nd, a **NEGRO MAN, ISAAC**, and his wife, **ELLEN**. He is a little less than 6 feet high; about 30 years old; very dark; thin, but strong. She stands just to his chin; weighs about 120 pounds; brown skin. Also, one **NEGRO GIRL, HANNAH**, and one **BABY**, name of **GIRL**. Owner forewarns all persons from hiring or harboring said slaves, his rightful property, as the law will be strictly enforced. Owner will pay a reward of $20 for each; total of $80 for the lot if they be secured in jail so that he gets them again.

Written this 5th day of November, 1850.

Franklin Williams
Edminton, Wake County,
North Carolina

"Papa!" Amanda said. "What if they . . . ?" Amanda had no time to finish her question. Mr. Meecker and Jake were no longer in the kitchen. Amanda saw them down at the end of the long side hallway. They had stopped in front of the closet and were turning the handle, trying to open the door!

"Locked" was all One-Word Jake said.

"What have you got inside here, John?" Charlie Meecker called out. "You know I have to have a look. Give us the key, John."

Papa's face had gone as gray as gunmetal. "Old clothes. Some rope," he said, the strength out of his voice. He sounded suddenly exhausted. "Not a thing in that closet, Charlie. Don't even know why I keep it locked."

"All the same, we got to take a look. The key, John."

Amanda's eyes twitched with nervousness. What if the girl named Hannah made a noise when Mr. Meecker opened the closet? What if the baby named Girl awakened and started to cry? What would happen? "The law will be strictly enforced." They would be "secured in jail so that he gets them again. . . . His rightful property."

And Papa? He would go to jail, too. For six months! That was what Mr. Meecker had told them. It was all too terrible to think about. But what could they do? Amanda's papa had said there was nothing left for them but to "hope and pray." That wasn't enough for Amanda. She had to think of something. She closed her eyes again. Her imagination began to work.

Six

And now Amanda had a plan. It was so clear she could see it.

Opening her eyes and turning her face away, she pinched her cheeks to redden them. Then, dancing up and down on the tips of her toes the way her little brother Thomas did when he was excited, Amanda resumed her playacting.

"I know, Papa! I know, Mama!" she said, tugging at her papa's pocket. "It's nearing Christmas, and it's a present for me. You've hidden it in the closet so as to surprise me. It's a new sled, isn't it, Papa? That's why the closet is locked. Oh, Papa, give Mr. Meecker the key so that he can open it and I may see. Give him the key, Papa!"

Papa stared at Amanda, startled and amazed, unable to speak. His mouth dropped open, as wide and as round as one of Mama's fancy little butter dishes.

"She *is* an excitable girl," Mr. Meecker said.

Mama cleared her throat. "That is so," she managed to say.

Amanda watched her papa. His hand trembled in his pocket.

Amanda took one last chance, a desperate and dangerous one. She slipped her hand into Papa's pocket, as if trying to get at the key. "Please, Papa?" she pretended to plead. "Give Mr. Meecker the key?"

Now Charlie Meecker knew exactly where the key was! His terrible snake eyes narrowed again and he stared straight at Papa's pocket. And now Amanda's playacting was finished. There was nothing more that she could do—except hope that it had worked.

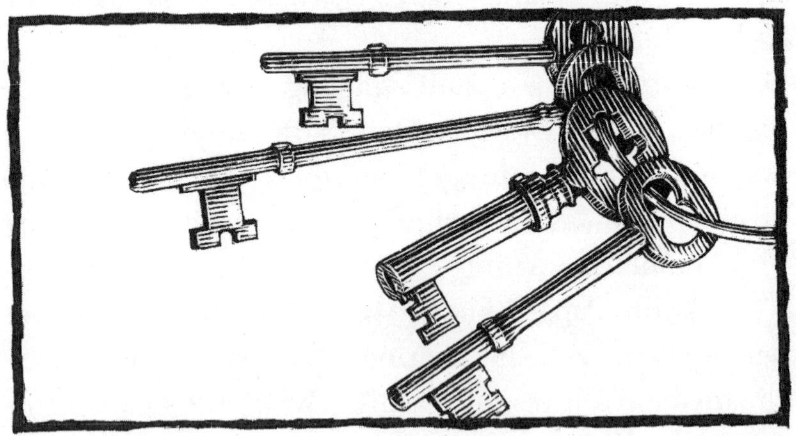

In the silence that followed, Amanda scarcely breathed. No one breathed, nor said a word. The only sound was the wind slapping at the house outside and the old house creaking and groaning in complaint. Everyone waited to see what would happen next.

"Christmas," Charlie Meecker finally said, shaking his head. "Well now, you know I should be doing my job, but . . . I'm not here to bring ruin to your occasions. I'm not one to spoil a surprise for a child. Never mind the key."

She'd done it! Amanda was dizzy with joy but careful to hide it.

"It's late, and I guess Jake and me have done enough

hunting for one night. We all of us best be getting to sleep. You're looking especially peaked, John. Here, want a hunk of this?" he asked, reaching now into his pocket and withdrawing a bit of the dried meat. "It'll revive you."

"No, thanks, Charlie, but you're right. I am a bit tired . . . what with unloading the wagon so late and all," Papa answered, his eyes fixed on Amanda, who was trying hard not to show how relieved she felt.

"And your little girl," Mr. Meecker continued, "well, she ought to be in bed, what with her nature. Too nervous and excitable, if you ask me."

"We didn't," Mama whispered under her breath, covering her words with a yawn.

"What was that you said, Amelia?" Charlie Meecker asked.

"Nothing, Charlie, Mr. Meecker. Nothing at all," Mama answered.

"Well, we'll be leaving you folks now. But remember, I'll be watching. Those runaways are about, probably trying to head north by the river. It's your duty to turn them in if you see them, John, no matter what your sympathies."

"Sympathies," One-Word Jake echoed.

"We'll be on the lookout," Papa promised, but Amanda noticed that Papa had crossed his fingers alongside his key pocket.

"Amelia," Mr. Meecker said, tipping his hat to her. "John. . . . Take carc of that girl of yours."

"Promise I will, Charlie," Papa said, uncrossing his fingers. "Promise I will."

Seven

"They've gone!" Papa whispered, closing the door and letting out his breath. "Amanda, you scared the senses out of me. That was too much of a chance you took! What if Charlie Meecker had taken the key and—"

"But he wouldn't have," Manda interrupted. "I don't know why, but somehow I knew. In my imagination, I could see everything. I could see that if Charlie Meecker thought it was a Christmas closet, he wouldn't open the door, and even though I don't like him, I could see that he wouldn't be so mean as to ruin Christmas."

"Still, Manda, what you did was dangerous. Now you know why I don't encourage your playacting! What you did was . . ." Papa shook his head, then, suddenly, his eyes lightened and he began to laugh. "What you did was . . . well . . . quite extraordinary. I guess I should keep my promise to Charlie Meecker."

"What promise?" Mama asked.

"My promise to take care of that girl of ours!" Papa said, smiling. "I think she deserves something special—a sucking candy from the cupboard. A peppermint one."

"Now?" Mama asked. "It's frightfully late."

"Right now," Papa commanded. "I know we shouldn't encourage her, but still, we have much to thank her for," he said, glancing toward the closet.

Amanda said nothing. She felt suddenly tired, her eyelids weighted. She was pleased to be silent at last and to have nothing to do but lean against Papa, cuddle Coey Yocks, and wait and watch while Mama went off to the highboy where candies were kept.

"You did a great deed this night for some worthy folk," Papa said.

"Thank you, Papa," Amanda answered sleepily.

"But I fear you've also learned a sad and grown-up lesson. Our world isn't always as just as it ought to be. Our laws are only as fair as the people who make them."

"It's men who make our laws," Mama said, handing Amanda her peppermint. "Perhaps one day women will!"

"That could be," Papa said, smiling at Mama. "But for now, until our country is a fairer one, we have to follow our conscience and do what is right by it, even if it means lying or practicing a deception. We have no choice. We have to help our fellow beings round their obstacles. Understand, Amanda?"

"No, Papa," Amanda answered, wondering if it was because she was so terribly tired. "I do not."

Papa's eyes squinted. He was thinking hard. "It's like when you play outside, and your Mama and I scold you for putting a stick in the way of a column of ants. There they are, going about their rightful business, on their way forward. Now they have to go around that stick you put there.

"We lied and deceived Charlie Meecker and poor old Jake tonight. All three of us did. But we did it because of an unfair law. We did it to remove a stick, an obstacle, cruelly and unfairly placed in the rightful path of our fellow human beings. We did it to help a fine family get to where they're going, to where they have every right to be."

"Where is that, Papa?" Amanda asked. Leaning against her father, her eyelids were so heavy now, they slipped shut. The adventure of the night, the lateness of the hour, the softness of Papa's voice—Amanda wanted to stay awake for his answer, but, despite her best effort, she drifted off to sleep.

In a peppermint-flavored dream, Amanda thought she heard Papa's answer. "To Canada, Amanda. To freedom."

Eight

It was the morning train, rumbling, rattling, clanking, and blowing its steam whistle that finally awakened Amanda from her strange dream. Jumping out of bed, she pulled the stool that Papa had made—and that Mama and she had decorated with stenciled flowers—to the window to look out.

Up by the house, it was quiet country, cows lowing, chickens scratching, and the meadow stretching leisurely out till it reached the high, weedy bluff that overlooked the river. Still and sleepy, the same as ever.

But down below, the world was wide awake, in the midst of motion and change. Just a year ago, the steel tracks of the new railroad had been laid, and now noisy trains sped along the edge of the Hudson River, belching and billowing pillows of smoke into the air, hurrying north from the city to someplace else, someplace far away, and then speeding back again.

The river bustled with activity, its rippled water plowed by small boats and barges, furrowed by ferries. A steamboat, the *Reindeer,* tooted its horn and raced up the river, flags flying, stacks spitting clouds of dark gray at the sky. Fast as it was, the new railroad was far faster. A steamboat might beat out another steamboat, but there was no way it could win against one of the new trains.

Out of sight, down in the quarries, men were hard at work cutting stone out of the ground. The sound of their pickaxes echoed off the craggy cliffs of the Palisades on the other side of the river.

Out beyond the meadow, the whole world seemed up and occupied. There were things to do, places to get to. No one stayed still. Everyone seemed to be in a hurry to be off to somewhere new. It was then that Amanda remembered . . .

Throwing off her nightclothes and pulling on her pantaloons, she slipped on her petticoat and her warmest brown frock and then laced up her boots. Ignoring the washstand, she took a quick glance in the looking glass, parted her hair, and patted her coral necklace for good health and good luck.

Thomas's bed was empty. Thomas, who had slept so peacefully through the noisy, disturbing dream that was last night, had probably risen early. But Amanda knew it wasn't a dream and that, this time, it wasn't her imagination. The runaway family that had appeared so mysteriously in the darkness was in her house this very minute, hiding . . . unless they had already departed! Now Amanda was in as much of a hurry as the world outside. She ran down the stairs to see if they were still there.

Nine

"Amanda!" Mama called out when she saw her. "No school for you today. We let you sleep. Thomas and Papa have done some of your chores. They have been to the henhouse for eggs and Papa has done the milking, but now you may help me with the serving and the laying of the table. We'll need service for seven this morning."

"Seven, Mama," Manda answered happily, opening the cupboard. They were still here! Amanda counted out seven plates and listened to the kitchen sing. Eggs bubbled and hissed in the skillet, bacon crackled and sizzled in the fry pan, biscuits breathed, and the teapot whistled along in harmony.

Thomas, his curly yellow hair like a little lion's mane, sat on the kitchen floor playing with his pair of wheeled wooden horses, pretending they were frolicking in the meadow. Manda would have known he'd done her chores for her even if Mama hadn't told her, for floating among his curls were the soft, speckled chicken feathers that decorated her own hair most mornings.

"Hello, Manda," Thomas said, putting up his full-moon face for a kiss.

"Hello, Tom Tom," Manda answered, kissing the moon.

Manda laid the kitchen table for company, wondering where the company was. Were they still inside the wall of the dark closet? Had they been hidden away the whole night?

"Put out some preserves . . . some honey also," Mama said. "A good-sized wedge of cheese might be fine, too. Yes, cheese," Mama added, as if she were thinking out loud. "And the apple butter."

It seemed they were going to feast this morning. Manda went to the larder and returned with the strawberry preserves she and Mama had put up a few months earlier, a jar of Bea Bailey's best honey, a large slice of cheddar cheese, and some of the smooth brown apple butter Manda and Mama had made just last week.

Papa came in. He sniffed the kitchen air and smiled. His tired eyes looked worried. Manda wondered if Papa had slept at all last night. "Ready?" Papa asked Mama.

"Ready," she answered. "You may commence serving, Manda."

Papa took a quick peek outside the window, closed the curtain, pulled the closet key from his pocket, and left the kitchen.

Manda took a deep breath and started dividing up the fluffy yellow eggs. She was just lifting the heavy fry pan off the cookstove to serve the bacon when, looking up, she saw the family of strangers standing timidly at the kitchen door.

Ten

"Come in. Come in," Mama invited.

"Come in. Come in," Thomas repeated from his position on the floor.

"You are welcome here and safe . . . as long as we keep a good watch," Mama said. "Sit down and fill yourselves with food and a bit of daylight. I'm sure it's dismal cold in that horrid little hiding place."

"Thank you, ma'am," the woman said, taking a tiny step forward, her eyes lowered so she looked only at the floor. "Let me help you with your work. My girl Hannah is a good worker, too. She helps cook in the white folks' kitchen. Do let her and me do some of the work. My family . . . well, we not used to being waited 'pon."

Amanda wondered at the way the woman named Ellen spoke. Her words were smooth and warm as summer wind. Her way was soft, but at the same time, strong. She reminded Amanda of someone special, someone in one of the stories she had read. Who could it be? She closed her eyes and tried to imagine. As soon as she did, she knew. Amanda opened her eyes and looked back at the woman. She was a princess! There could be no doubt. A princess from a dark and distant land.

"Please," Mama was saying. Wiping her hands on her apron, she approached the princess. "You must let us wait on you. You've had a long and difficult trip. Sit down with us now, rest and eat." And Mama took Princess Ellen by the arm, led her to the table, and sat her down so that she could more easily cradle the baby, awake now and gurgling in her arms.

The tall, thin man named Isaac—her husband—sat next to her. Like Princess Ellen's, his eyes stared only at the floor.

"You've already met our son, Thomas," Mama said. "Thomas, stand up and greet our guests properly."

Thomas stood up. "Properly," he said, extending a chubby arm.

"And now meet Amanda, my daughter. Manda, meet

Mr. and Mrs. Williams and their daughters, Hannah and Girl."

Amanda smiled a small smile. All of a sudden she felt shy and nervous. She put her lips together to form the words "Pleased to meet you," but before she could do it, the girl named Hannah spoke.

"Howdie, Missie Amanda," she said brightly, and curtsied.

"How do you do yourself, Hannah," Amanda said, so surprised to be curtsied at, she forgot her sudden shyness. "You don't have to curtsy and you don't have to call me Miss. Amanda's fine enough. Manda, for short, is what most people call me." And then, Amanda held the skirt of her frock aside and curtsied back to the girl.

From his station by the window, Papa smiled, but the girl named Hannah startled. "Oh!" she cried, and covered her mouth with her hand to hide a nervous laugh.

"Where we come from, white folk don't curtsy to black," the man named Isaac explained, lifting his eyes and stealing a glance at Amanda. "And it sure is true that they don't ever, no *never,* serve and wait 'pon us."

"Well," Papa said, "while you're in this house, it is our aim to treat you right, take care of you, and give you a chance to rest and restore yourselves until you have to resume your journey."

At that, Princess Ellen bent her head. Was she crying, Amanda wondered, as she watched Hannah move silently toward her mother and reach her arm around her mother's neck to comfort her. She was.

Mama's face reddened. "No cause to worry yourself now."

"Here," Amanda said, offering her handkerchief.

"Thank you kindly," the princess said, accepting it and looking up at Amanda with a smile.

"My goodness," Mr. Williams exclaimed, "I do hope we can return the favor someday."

"You will, one day. If not to us, then to another in need," Mama said. "But now, everyone sit, please. I am certain that Charlie Meecker has not yet finished with us, so while we have the time, let us eat together. But first, John will say grace."

"Good Father," Papa said, bowing his head as, slowly, shyly, they all joined hands in a circle around the table. "For good food, for good company, we are grateful."

"Amen," they all agreed, except for Manda, who was busy with her own grace. Good Father, she silently prayed. For Charlie Meecker—a good cold. One for One-Word Jake as well—*big* ones that will keep both of them tucked up in bed for at least a week or two!

"Thank you," she whispered into her chest. "Amen."

Eleven

Manda had cleared the last of the dishes from the table, and Hannah, insisting that she be allowed to help, had scraped them in preparation for washing, when Papa surprised Manda with some wonderful words.

"Manda, you are excused from chores today. Take Hannah up to your bedchamber. You may talk and do whatever you wish, only do it quietly. But Manda, no play-acting! You need to keep your wits about you at all times and not take any chances. Hannah, you must be sure to stay away from the window lest anyone be spying on us, and do *not*, under any circumstances, go outside. Thomas, you stay with us. Your rolling horses await you. Manda," Papa beckoned.

"Yes, Papa?"

Papa lowered his voice to a whisper. "If I give a whistle, you must come quickly so Hannah can go back into hiding. Then, fast as you are able to run, you are to take Thomas out to play hoop down in the meadow, far away from the house, so that he doesn't give anything away. We are courting disaster when little ones with large-sized mouths know grown-up secrets.

"Mr. and Mrs. Williams—Ellen and Isaac, if I may call you that—stay out here as long as possible by the fire and keep warm. I shall keep my watch and whistle if I see anyone, then it will be quick into the closet with all of you. That leaves only you, Amelia, with a heap of kitchen work to do on your own, without Amanda to help."

"I can manage, John," Mama said, smiling.

"Mrs. Van Dorn?" Princess Ellen began.

"Amelia," Mama corrected.

"Miss Amelia . . ." Princess Ellen began again.

Mama sighed.

"Where I come from," Princess Ellen explained, "we always say Mister or Miss when speaking to white folk."

"Then I shall call you Miss Ellen," Mama said, "for we are equals."

Princess Ellen shook her head in what looked like wonder. "All right then, but if we are equals, I will be doing my equal share of cleaning up!"

Mama smiled. "I accept," she said. "Only who will watch the baby?"

Princess Ellen laughed. "Girl will watch *us*. When I'm out in the fields picking cotton for Master, she rides high on my back, like a perching bird, looking every which way and listening to my song, just as Hannah did once, and Sylvie and Samuel did, too, before they were taken."

"Sylvie and Samuel, they . . . our two little babies that passed on," Isaac Williams explained softly.

The kitchen fell suddenly silent, the only sound the clock on the shelf *tick, tick, ticking* bits of time away.

Mama's eyelids fluttered. She said nothing, and no one but Amanda seemed to notice. Manda knew that Mama was thinking of *her* two babies—Manda's little brother Peter, with cheeks as smooth as pudding, who had died of scarlet fever a few winters ago when he was little bigger than Thomas was now, and the new baby named Elizabeth who had come, like a crocus, early last spring and had not even lived long enough to be held in Mama's arms.

"Girl will watch from my back and see how well and how fast we clean up together," Princess Ellen continued. "One day she will be free in Canada to do her own chores for herself. She and my Hannah will have no master, no mistress. They will be master and mistress of themselves." Ellen's soft voice deepened till it was strong and rich as Papa's coffee.

"Amen," Papa said with emotion. "May it be so. But now, off with you, Manda. We grown-ups have things to talk about, while we have the time. While *you* have the time, take your new friend upstairs."

New friend, Manda thought. The two words sounded good together. Shyly, Manda reached for Hannah's hand, and led her up the stairs.

Twelve

"Sit on the floor with me," Manda said. "Let us do as my Papa said and stay low and away from the window in case the constable, Charlie Meecker, or One-Word Jake sneak up and try to spy on us."

"All right, Miss Amanda. I mean, Manda for short," Hannah said.

Manda laughed. "It's true that I *am* on the short side, but if you keep calling me 'Manda for short,' I'll just have to call you 'Hannah for long,' for you are on the long side."

Now Hannah laughed, a laugh that was full and lilting, a laugh that seemed to pour out of her like there was no end to it. "I *am* on the long side, just like my pappy," Hannah said proudly. "When I was tiny, no bigger than a minute, even then, they say I looked like a long dark stick of sugarcane. I'll try to get used to calling you just plain Manda, but Miss Mand—I mean, just Manda, I'm afraid it's gonna take me a time or two."

"Take your time, Hannah-for-long," Manda said, smiling. "But for now, hold on to my Coey Yocks. Since today is special, I will take Madam Cora down from her shelf so that we can play with her. She is my fancy doll. My uncle Oliver, who is a businessman and very rich, bought her for me in a shop in London, England. He told me to be very careful with her. She is made of wax and very, very delicate, so I play with her only at special times and never outdoors. The heat from the sun would melt her."

"She is just like my Miss Becca," Hannah said, as Manda carefully placed Madam Cora on the floor beside Hannah and Coey Yocks. "I have to keep *her* out of the sun, too."

"Is Miss Becca your doll?" Hannah asked, reaching for Uncle Oliver's tiny tea set with the painted pink roses on it.

"Oh, no!" Hannah said, more laughter spilling out. "Miss Rebecca Williams is no doll, though she wants as much care. She is the daughter of my master, twelve years old, and live as you and me. She is my mistress who owns me—I belong to her."

"Belong to her?" Manda asked. "Did you say she *owns* you?" Manda had never imagined she'd meet someone who would use such words about herself.

"Yes, she chose me for herself alone," Hannah said, pausing. "She's a delicate one and lazy, Miss Becca, but not so bad as some. Only once ever did she have me whupped."

At Hannah's last word Manda nearly dropped her tea set. Sometimes, Papa said, it was necessary to whip Old Harley to get him going, but *he* was a saddle horse. Even so, Papa hated doing it. "Why did she have you whipped? What did you do? It must have been something awfully terrible!"

"Oh, yes, something very bad," Hannah answered, with assurance.

"What was it? What did you do?" Manda asked.

"Oh, I can't tell you that. I couldn't," Hannah said, looking frightened.

And though Manda ached to know the terrible thing Hannah had done, she held off asking. What could it have been? Manda tried to imagine, but she couldn't.

"But always else," Hannah continued, "I was smart and did all the chores Miss Becca told me to do."

"What chores?" Manda asked.

Hannah sighed. "Well . . . whenever the sky dripped rain, carry Miss Becca's umbrella over her head, so she stay dry. Whenever the sun smiled warm, carry Miss Becca's umbrella so she stay cool. In the morning, put on Miss Becca's fine clothes. Late in the day, when it sticky-fly hot and time for her nap, stand by Miss Becca's bed and fan her till she asleep and my tired arms do tingle like they stuck full with sewing needles. In the shadow of the afternoon, shell corn, peel taters in the kitchen with Aunt Viney and Uncle Jim, th' other house slaves who are my friends. And *sometime* . . . when the Big House is quiet and the white folks asleep, go in the library, take down the books, and . . . and . . . and . . . dust them." Hannah's voice grew quiet. She whispered and looked fearfully up at Manda when she spoke of the library and the books.

Manda scarcely knew what to say. Hannah used words in such a special way, as pretty as a poem in one of Uncle Oliver's books, but underneath those words she spoke about things that weren't pretty, things Manda had only vaguely heard about and never really imagined.

Hannah's nervous eyes darted to the shelf where

Manda kept the precious books Uncle Oliver had given her, then to Manda, and back again to the bookshelf.

"Would you like to read one of my books?" Manda asked, guessing at what Hannah was thinking and jumping up. Standing before her bookshelf, Manda chose one of her favorites, a book of fairy tales, and placed it on the floor next to Hannah. But instead of picking it up, Hannah withdrew her hands and sat on them.

"Don't worry," Manda reassured her. "Even though it's another of my uncle Oliver's gifts, this one won't break. You don't have to worry. It isn't like Madam Cora; it's a *book*! You can touch it, and read it, and even borrow it while you're here. If you have to go and hide again, it will help pass the time quite wonderfully, if there's enough light in that horrible old closet. Here, take it," Manda said, trying to hand it to Hannah.

But Hannah shrank from Manda's reach, and when Manda tried to place the book in her lap, she trembled.

"Really, Hannah, you may borrow it. Do you know the story about the twelve dancing princesses?"

"No," Hannah answered.

"Well, it's a good one. It's in this book. Here . . . you may read it."

"I can't."

"Of course you may."

"But I *can't*!" Hannah insisted.

"Why can't you?" Manda asked, growing impatient.

"I can't," Hannah said slowly, "because I don't know *how* to read."

Hannah's eyes stared at the floor now, the way her mother's had when she first came into the kitchen. She didn't raise them to look at Manda. She looked ashamed.

Everything stopped inside Manda while she tried to understand. Even lazy Silas Bean who sat next to Manda in school and never paid the slightest bit of attention could read a little! "But *why*, Hannah? Why can't you read? Did no one ever teach you?"

Hannah shook her head. "You better never be found trying to learn how to read where I come from," she answered softly. "Master say, if he catch anyone with a book, they be whipped till they're . . ." Hannah trailed off. "Or worse . . . sent away. *No* one allowed to learn letters! It's the same 'most everywhere, not just on Master Williams's plantation, though I did hear of a master a couple counties down who 'lows his slaves to learn letters."

"But why?" Manda asked again, trying to imagine a

world where no one was permitted to read or write. Manda shivered to think of it. "Why?" she repeated for the third time.

"Mammy say reading is freedom. Pappy say the thoughts in books are powerful strong, stronger even than chains. He say Master is 'fraid of the power of words."

And all of a sudden Manda knew what Hannah had done that had gotten her whipped. "You tried to read, didn't you, Hannah?" she asked. "In the master's library. Is that why Miss Becca had you whipped?"

Hannah nodded shyly. "I opened a big book in the library, 'stead of dusting it," Hannah whispered. "I wanted so bad to figure out the lines of letters and what they were saying. But I couldn't."

"Hannah," Manda cried out in sympathy.

"Hush!" Hannah said, and, glancing over her shoulder as if to check that someone might be watching, she dug deep inside her pocket and withdrew a torn piece of sackcloth and a charred bit of wood. "Look," she whispered, and there on the floor of Manda's room, carefully, painfully, she drew two parallel black lines up and down on the floor and then crossed them in the middle with the coal to make an *H.* Then, she drew two lines that met at the top and crossed them to make an *A.* She drew an *N,* and then another *N,* and then another *A,* and then a final *H.*

HANNAH

"Hannah!" Manda cried out, and hugged her.

"Shhhhh!" Hannah said, and with the sackcloth in one hand and the skirt of her dress in the other, she nervously erased her name. "Viney taught me," she whispered. "She knows a few letters. She say I'm smart. She say, one day I will know even more than her."

"You will, Hannah-for-long, you will. I will teach you," Manda said, making a solemn promise. "We'll start today."

Thirteen

"I *hate* your Miss Becca!" Manda said, banging her foot on the floor in anger.

"Shouldn't," Hannah said. "Mammy say hate is poison. Miss Becca don't mean to be mean. 'S just the way things are."

"Miss Becca? Have you always worked for, I mean, belonged to her?" Manda asked, uncomfortable with the words she was suddenly forced to use.

"Always and ever I belonged to Master, but the last two years I do for Miss Becca. Before that, I live with my family and help in the fields. But ever since the day Miss Becca choose me to wait on her, I live in the Big House where Master himself live. That choosing day was one sad day! My mammy Ellen cried so, and my pappy was cross 'cause I would never be 'llowed to live with them ever again, but they were happy, too."

"Why?" Manda asked.

" 'Cause I had luck. Now I would sleep on a cloud-soft bed instead of a plain pallet, and have shoes and clean clothes and an apron stiff with starch, good food, too—biscuits and butter twice a week, and ham!

"But I'll tell you, Manda," Hannah said proudly, "I never forget my family. Sometimes at night I did sneak that ham and biscuits down to the cabin for my fam'ly. I hid it all in the hollow of a tree and got the word to Mammy where to find it. And, sometimes, on dark nights when the moon was away on holiday and my heart was half and lonely, I did sneak out late and meet Mammy and Pappy in the allées under the live oak trees. And we did smile and speak secrets and listen and learn night sounds, not forgetting to look out for Big Man Rumpus, that mean man overseer always swinging his leather strap. And Mammy, and Pappy, too, would whisper stories and dreams of freedom in my ear."

"You are brave, Hannah-for-long," Manda said, full of admiration.

"I know, Manda-for-short!" Hannah laughed. "I am! Even Big Man Rumpus and his whip can't scare me. My mammy says I have the freedom spirit. Mammy, Pappy, even Girl. We *all* have it."

"You do, Hannah, you do. You are the bravest person I've ever known. But Big Man Rumpus . . . how did you ever get away?"

"Well, that's a long story," Hannah answered.

"Tell me!" Manda said.

Fourteen

"First, drink some tea," Manda offered, pretending to pour some for Hannah. Manda wished it was real, and that she had real cake and cookies to give her. "Take Madam Cora. Uncle Oliver told me not to let anyone touch her but me, but you may hold her."

"No, thank you. She too fussy for me, but I like your Coey Yocks."

"I do, too," Manda said, "because you can play with her." Manda took Coey Yocks and tossed her up to the ceiling. She wished she and Hannah could go outside and toss Coey Yocks up to the sky. "Catch!" Manda called out as Coey Yocks spiraled down, turning wonderful somersaults in the air.

Hannah raised one long, thin arm and easily caught Coey Yocks around her stuffed-cotton middle.

"Hannah, you may play with Coey Yocks all you want," Manda said importantly, "only first tell me how you got away and what made you decide to try and go."

"It was on account of my birthday. A little before this Christmas I'll be ten years old."

"That's how old I am, too!" Manda said, excitedly. "Only last month I turned ten. Ten feels so much older and better than nine! I think it's my favorite age of all ages to be."

“It’s not my favorite age,” Hannah said, and there wasn’t one drop of laughter spilling out of her. “Where *I* come from ten is bad . . . on account of Hiring Day.”

“What’s that?” Manda asked.

“The first and the *worst* day of January!” Hannah said, with feeling. “The day when Master can hire us slaves out for a whole year if he choose to. Aunt Viney heared Master say, now that I soon be ten and nearly grown, quick as Hiring Day come, he gonna get Miss Becca a new girl to wait on her and hire me out to a Missus Crawford, on another plantation, way far along in Georgia. Viney, with her two good ears, say she hear Missus Crawford is a mean old lady who’ll whup you for the smile on your face or the sparkle in your eye. And then, Aunt Viney hear something even worse!”

“What’s that?” Manda asked, with dread.

“She hear Master talking ’bout selling my pappy for cash, saying he would fetch a fine price, maybe near to a thousand dollars, for he is strong and so good a carpenter that he can make almost anything out of wood. Viney say Master going to take my pappy over to Charleston and put him on the auction block and see how much he can get for him, and then we will never, *ever* see him again. So, Pappy and Mammy decided it was time, right then, to ’range a trip on that Underground Railroad we keep on hearing about. Like I told you, we have the freedom spirit!”

Manda could barely breathe. “But how did you get away?”

“Aunt Viney, she help us hatch a plan. She tell Master she in the mood to cook him a special supper. Then she cook pork and greens and chicken and pie, and Uncle Jim and me, we help her. Then Viney wait until darkness and fill Master full of food and lots of drink so he so sleepy he can't hardly get up. Then she call Big Man Rumpus, tell him carry Master up the stairs to his bed. But first, she slip Big Man Rumpus some drink for himself along with her tasty spoon bread, like she doing him a favor, and when he good and sleepy, Viney start to singing, 'The gospel train is comin'/I hear it just at hand/I hear the wheels a-movin'/A rumblin' through the land./Get on board, little children/Get on board, little children/Get on board, little children/There's room for many a more.'

"The minute I hear Viney singing that song, I know it is a signal. I am upstairs with Miss Becca fixing her for bed, hoping she fall asleep fast so I can leave. When I hear that song I get so scared, my face turn the color of cooked collards. Miss Becca, she say, 'Hannah, you look sick. Stay away from me. Go down to Viney and tell her you got the fever.' So I hurry away even earlier than I plan . . . but not to Viney!"

"Where did you go?" Manda asked, with scarcely any breath left to ask her question.

"I hurry to the meeting place to find Mammy and Pappy and Girl. Mammy give Girl the special drops to make her sleep, so she not cry out, and we sneak away. Down through the thicket we go, the bushes scratching at my legs, old hoot owls hollering in the trees, crickets hissing and sassing us all the way and me so scared, I feel like a mess of frogs are a-flopping in my innards! We go far out to the end of Master Williams's plantation, where the big stream is. That's where Uncle Jim has hung us up some cornbread in a tree for our trip. We walk in the water so no dogs can sniff us, staying close to the edge, under the trees, so the mean man pattyrollers can't spy us. Those pattyrollers, they *always* on the lookout for runaways."

"Why?" Manda whispered.

"'S their job. If they or their sniffing dogs catch you, they can run you up a tree, and when you brought down, they . . . well, Manda, I can't talk 'bout that!"

Manda shook her head back and forth, trying hard, for once, to stop her imagination.

"Far upstream," Hannah continued, "a kindly white man sneak us a boat and a blanket, and we row upriver. When the sky grow light and start to blush like Miss Becca, it's morning and time to hide. We come ashore and push the boat out on the water, leaving the blanket behind so if someone see it, they think we are drowned and dead. Then we find a hiding place, eat our cornbread, and fall dead-dog asleep till darkness come."

"And then?" Manda asked.

"And then we walk all night, following along under that North Star, till our feet feel like they made of mush, 'specially my pappy's, cause he don't have shoes."

"How did you keep on going?"

"In my head I keep singing that song I know about holding on."

"What song?"

Hannah looked shyly at Manda and then, very softly, began to sing. "'Hold on. . . . Hold on. Keep your hand on the plow, hold on.' We pass many days hiding, and many nights walking, till we get to a boggy ol' place in Virginia that folks call the Dismal Swamp. There we meet another runaway who calls himself Freeman Jones. He is brave, he is smart, and he is a conductor on the Underground Railroad. He steals us some bread and a lick of molasses and shows us a way 'cross the Mason-Dixon line to the free state of Pennsylvania, where we *still* not free."

"Why not?" Manda asked.

"On account of that new law and Master Williams's slave catchers. He put out papers that say we runaways and his property. Any that catch us will get a reward."

"Charlie Meecker, our constable—just last night he left one of those papers here with my papa," Manda interrupted. "I read it!"

"Nowhere is safe, so we hide behind a woodpile, so tired, we think to give up. Then, like an angel, a Quaker lady with a big white bonnet 'pears and whispers soft to us, 'Come out.' She takes us in her wagon, under her quilt to her house, and hides us just like your family does. And this lady is so small and quiet, not a one suspects her, but just like your mammy and pappy, she is one of the stationmasters on the Underground Railroad."

Just then, Hannah and Manda heard the midday train in the distance, rumbling and clacking up the tracks. Manda took Hannah's hand and led her to the stool. Standing carefully away from the window, they could steal a glance outside, past the big tree that grew close to the house, and down along the river. Out in the open, loud and proud and unafraid to make as much noise as it needed to, the dark train screamed out its warning: "I'm long and strong and everyone else better step aside!" Then it whistled and snorted and hurried away.

Hidden away for the first time in her life, Manda felt suddenly trapped and restless. Unable to go outside with Hannah, she realized how lucky she had always been. As long as she finished her chores, she was free to come and go, here or there, as she wished. Now, for the first time, she was not free. She was stuck inside, forced to be vigilant and careful. Was this how it felt to be Hannah—always vigilant, always careful, *never* able to be out in the open? The feeling of restlessness in Manda grew bigger.

"What happened after the Quaker lady hid you?" Manda asked, pulling Hannah safely away from the window and sitting her down again on the floor by Madam Cora and Coey Yocks. "How did you get here?"

"We have one more stop on the Railroad, a barn in New Jersey, and then the man your pappy knows comes and puts us in his wagon and keeps us hid in his grain sacks and brings us to your house. And that is my story so far, till we have to leave and go along again on our way to Canada."

"How I wish you and your family could stay here, Hannah!"

"Pappy say, till this new law was made, we could have, but not now. We not safe. We must get to Canada. There, Girl can get her name! Mammy's been waiting for Canada to give Girl her freedom name. And me? Well, I'm gonna get a new name, too! All my life, people call me Hannah Williams, Master Williams's slave girl. Now, people call me Hannah Williams, *runaway* girl. But soon, Manda, soon, I'm gonna call me Hannah Canada, *free person*!"

"Hannah Canada?" Manda said, testing the way the new name felt in her mouth. "I like it. It suits you. I shall call you Hannah Canada from now on."

Manda closed her eyes and tried to imagine Hannah in Canada, free. She saw Hannah out in the open, sitting high up in a tree, smiling. She saw Hannah running through a meadow, laughing her special laugh. The tree Manda imagined Hannah in, looked like one of the trees in Papa's orchard. The meadow looked like the meadow outside Manda's window. Manda realized that Hannah had never had even a single minute of freedom in her whole life! The feeling of restlessness in Manda turned to anger. Why did Hannah have to wait until she got to Canada? Manda wished she could let Hannah into her imagination, so Hannah could see what she could see, so she could show Hannah freedom.

Suddenly Manda had an idea. She opened her eyes, so excited she could hardly speak. She could give Hannah a present—a glimpse of what she had just seen in her imagination. "Hannah," she said breathlessly. "Come with me. I want to show you freedom!"

"What do you mean?" Hannah asked.

"We'll go outside."

"Outside?" Hannah repeated, nervously.

"For only a short time. Then we'll come back. No one will even realize we're not here. We'll climb out my window and down my tree. I'll take you through the meadow. We can go far away from the house, where no one will see us, to the orchard and climb in the trees. Maybe I'll even"—Manda lowered her voice—"show you the secret passageway I found. We'll come back so quickly, no one will know we were gone."

"But Manda," Hannah said, "it's daylight. What if someone sees me?"

"They won't, because we'll be ever so careful."

"Are you *sure* no one will see us?" Hannah asked. "Those men who came last night . . . what if they come back again?"

Manda was too excited to listen or think. Grabbing Coey Yocks, she looked out her window to be certain no one was there. Then she swung herself out onto the oak tree. "Come on, Hannah Canada," she called out in a whisper. "Freedom. Let me show it to you."

"Freedom," Hannah whispered longingly. She paused for only a moment and then whispered, "Here I come!" Hurrying after Manda, Hannah smiled, then she, too, stepped out through the open window.

Fifteen

Down on the ground, Manda looked this way and that, more fearful that her father might see them as he kept his kitchen window watch than that Charlie Meecker might appear.

Hannah teetered on a branch above.

"Jump!" Manda whispered from below.

Hannah jumped, landing with a soft thump on the ground.

Had anyone heard? Manda and Hannah stayed still, listening. No noise from inside. "Follow me!" Manda breathed.

Crawling along the side of the house, frightened by the crunch of every leaf and the crack of every twig, Manda hurried in the direction of the barn.

"Duck," Hannah whispered to Manda when they made it into the high grass. She put her hand on Manda's back and pressed down on it. "Do like me. I know how to keep hidden. Gotta stay low."

Manda nodded and hunched down, managing, nevertheless, to move quickly. No matter how fast Manda hurried, Hannah stayed perfectly at her heels, so close she felt like Manda's shadow.

"Chickens!" Hannah whispered in warning, surprising Manda. It was almost as if Hannah knew Papa's farm

better than Manda did. With just the one word and a quick yank of Manda's shoulder, Hannah quickly changed their direction and steered Manda away from the noisy brood.

Only Golden saw them and set to complaining. The other chickens continued their pecking, never noticing the two girls as they scurried nervously past them.

Hannah and Manda were already a distance from the house, but not yet far enough away for safety, so Manda continued on, resuming the lead, through the tall, dry, end-of-autumn grass that was the uncut portion of the meadow.

Manda's legs felt cramped from crouching. Every part of her seemed to itch from the tickling meadow. Every few minutes, Hannah reached for Manda's arm to stop her. "Time to listen," she instructed. Together they waited silently, straining to hear stray sounds—human ones like those Charlie Meecker or One-Word Jake might make. Then, when Hannah nodded, they'd hurry on again. Continuing across the meadow, the only noises Manda heard were her own breath and, farther off, the raucous squawk of ravens arguing with one another.

Manda had intended to take Hannah to the apple orchard, but now she thought the woods might be safer. "Are you all right to go farther?" she whispered to Hannah.

Hannah's smile, as bright and sunny as Manda had imagined it would be, was her answer.

Manda kept on, hands held out ahead of her, play-acting. She pretended she was a ship, parting the high sea of grass with her prow. If she navigated correctly, she and her precious passenger would land, safely, at the edge of the woods that bordered the meadow.

And then, finally, they were there. The shadowy, windy woods whistled an invitation. "Come on!" Manda called excitedly to Hannah. She spoke quietly, but no longer in a whisper. "We're safe and out of sight here. Bet I can climb higher than you!" Manda teased, grabbing on to a tree limb and swinging herself up.

Hannah, at her heels, merely smiled her sunny smile. "Higher than me? Let's see."

Sixteen

Manda scrambled halfway up the tree, then paused to locate Hannah.

"Up here," a taunting voice called out.

From high above, Hannah waved to Manda.

"How did you get up so fast?" Manda asked, full of admiration. Hannah didn't answer. Instead, she climbed higher and higher, moving gracefully from branch to branch with only the slightest effort. At last she stopped and, perching proudly like a queen on a throne, sat suspended between two narrow, forklike branches, smiling down on Manda. "Pretend you are the queen and I am your faithful servant," Manda called up to her.

Hannah laughed her lilting laugh. "*I* am no queen, but my grandmammy was!"

"A queen?"

"Yes, a queen, name of Djuna, back in Africa. My mammy told me so. When Mammy was not so old as me, slavers came and stole her from her mammy, and even though my mammy was a young one, she has not forgotten her Djuna. She say she was tall and straight, quiet as a deer, beautiful, and the color of night."

"I *knew* it! I knew your mother was a princess!" Manda said triumphantly, "and that makes you a princess, too, Hannah."

Hannah just laughed.

"You are like one of the twelve dancing princesses in the book I tried to show you back at the house! Here, Princess Hannah, catch!" Manda called, and bobbing on her branch, she tossed Coey Yocks up through the upper branches of the tree toward Hannah and the sky.

Hannah leaned out from her throne and caught the doll as she flew upward. "Here she comes down again," Hannah called to Manda.

Manda balanced carefully on her branch, reached out, and nearly falling from the tree, caught Coey Yocks on her way down. "This will be our game," Manda said. "Toss-in-a-tree. Ready, Hannah?"

But Hannah didn't answer. She didn't seem to hear. She sat, high upon her throne, the last leaves of autumn caught in her hair like a golden crown, gazing off at what Manda imagined to be her kingdom. She looked somehow different than she had before, and the longer Manda looked up at her, the more Manda wondered what that difference was. And then, finally, Manda knew. Hannah looked peaceful. She looked long and still and quiet as the river did when no one was on it.

It was then that Manda remembered her promise. . . . Quick as a squirrel, she scrambled down the tree to the ground. She found a good stick. There was something important she and Hannah had to do. She was sorry, but she had to disturb the peaceful princess.

"Hannah," Manda called out softly. "Come with me."

Seventeen

Manda, carrying the stick, and Hannah, carrying Coey Yocks, crept out of the woods together, through the apple orchard, stopping along the way to gather skirtloads of anything that caught their fancy—windfall apples, dried corn husks, thistles and chestnuts, vines and berries and bits of grass.

Manda was watchful and alert now that they were more exposed in the orchard. Back in the meadow again, hidden in the high grass, she steered them toward the clearing at the edge of the high bluff that overlooked the river.

There they unloaded their skirts and, far away from anyone, stood together, looking about.

The world, so curious and wonderful, spread deliciously before them like a feast. Across the river, a buttery sun browned the cliffs of the Palisades until they looked like large, jagged slices of gingerbread. The sky seemed peppered with blackbirds, the river spiced with boats. Even the railroad tracks gleamed and sparkled like ice fresh from the icehouse.

"I feel like I can taste everything," Hannah said, the tip of her tongue moving across her lips. "In Canada, I will," she added, with determination.

Manda smiled. "But first, Hannah, I promised you

something. I promised I would teach you the alphabet."

"Now?" Hannah asked. "Here?"

"Yes. It will be easy. You already know how to write your name. That means you already know three letters—*a, h,* and *n.* So we can start with *b,*" Manda said, reaching for her stick.

"Wait," Hannah said, stilling Manda's hand with hers. "It's an awful big present you're giving me, Manda. Before you—"

"Oh, it's not a present," Manda interrupted. "It's just me teaching you letters—how to write them, and maybe read them."

Hannah uttered not a single word. She only looked deep into Manda's eyes, and Manda knew she'd been corrected.

"Before you give me your present, I want to give *you* one," Hannah said. "Watch," she instructed, and gathered up some of the treasures they had carried in their skirts. Manda watched as Hannah took the corn husk, a few twigs, and some vine and yanked and twisted them together into what began to look like a body. Then, using a stick and a rock as a hammer, Hannah poked a hole in the chestnut and added it . . . to make a head. She braided grasses to make hair and tied the braids onto the chestnut with vine. Last, she burst berries and colored the corn husk that was now a skirt red, and drew lips, two eyes, and a nose on the chestnut head. In a matter of minutes, she had created a doll. "For you, Manda. From me, Hannah."

Manda held the doll and turned it slowly in her hands to examine it from every side. "It's perfect," she breathed. "I will keep it forever. Thank you," she said simply.

"Now . . . *my* present," Hannah said, with excitement. "There are a great many letters in that alphabet. I know. Viney told me. Even so, I intend to learn them all! Can we begin?"

"Yes!" Manda said, laughing at Hannah's impatience. Using her foot as an eraser, she smoothed out the earth in the bald spot of the bluff so there were no footprints. Then she took up her stick to begin. . . .

Eighteen

"Watch!" Manda said, just the way Hannah had, and drew a large *B* in the earth. "The line goes straight down from the top, then you attach two half-circle bumps, and you get a capital *B* for *Boat.* If we have time, I'll teach you small *b,* but for now, this will have to do. You try now."

Hannah took the stick and carefully, deliberately, drew a large and perfect *B.* *"B!"* she proclaimed.

"Good," Manda said. "When you read it, make the sound that begins *boat* and *boy.*"

"*Boat* and *boy,*" Hannah repeated slowly and thoughtfully.

"Now *C,*" Manda said, erasing her own and Hannah's *B.* "A half-circle looking to the right. *C* is for *cat,* but also *circle.* Easy to write, harder to read, because it has two sounds, one hard, one soft."

"One hard, one soft," Hannah repeated, and drew a splendid *C.*

And so the lesson continued, with *D* for *dog* and *E* for *Ellen* and then *F.* "A straight line down," Manda said, "a top like a shelf, and then, halfway down, a half shelf. *F* is for . . ." Manda stopped to think.

"Freedom," Hannah answered, and erasing Manda's *F,* proudly drew her own.

"So it is," Manda said, smiling. "Now *G.* This one's a lot harder to write than some of the others. You start at the top and you . . ."

Just then she detected a sound in the distance. Horses. Lots of them. Horses and . . . what was that second sound? A dog barking!

"Hannah! We have to hide!"

"Where?" Hannah asked.

Manda closed her eyes, trying to think. The clatter of horses' hooves and the terrible barking were close, too close for them to get back to the house. They were out in the open . . . where they never should have been. It was all her fault, Manda's racing mind scolded her. Horses, her mind screamed. A dog! No one but herself to blame. Too risky to hide in the meadow. Need someplace else. Someplace hidden away. But where? *Where?* Manda's mind began finally to work. The Hole. . . . Manda opened her eyes.

"Follow me," she whispered to Hannah, seizing her hand. "Hurry!"

Nineteen

Racing, running, yanking Hannah this way and that, Manda skirted the edge of the meadow, aware that they were running a risk out in the open, but eager to get to her destination by the shortest, most direct route.

Behind the house, beyond the barn, a narrow path wove its way back into the woods. Manda headed down it, aiming them toward the Sad Place, the small grove of evergreens—pine and spruce and hemlock—where the babies, Peter and Elizabeth, were buried, a hand-carved marker on their graves made from the granite that workers cut from the quarries in town.

Usually, Manda stopped to place some flowers she had gathered on the graves—daisies in the summer, asters in the fall—and to sit for a while on the hand-hewn bench Papa had made. Holding Coey Yocks close, she'd think about the babies, but today she pulled Hannah past with barely a glance, certain that Peter and Elizabeth would understand.

"Where are we going?" Hannah asked in a tight voice.

Manda hardly knew how to answer, so she didn't. They were headed for the mysterious dark hole at the end of the path, the one Papa had hidden from sight, covering it over with a large pile of brambly brush so that no one would find it. The Hole was the second place Papa had told Manda never, under any conditions, ever to enter.

Papa, Manda was discovering, had secrets—lots of them—but Manda had a secret, too. Hers was that she had disobeyed Papa, more than once. Unlike the closet, the Hole had no lock on it, and so one afternoon, Manda had snuck down to the clearing, pushed the tangle of branches aside, and climbed inside. She discovered it was more than a hole. It was a tunnel—a secret passageway.

Dark and damp as it was, Manda had detected a small circle of light at its end. Pretending to be a miner searching for precious metals, she had made her way through the long, dark tunnel. Creeping and crawling and shivering at the thought of bats and the teasing tickle of unseen creatures, she had eventually reached the end. Here, the secret passageway opened, and Manda stepped out into the daylight. She was at the top of a steep hill. A brook began there, and Manda followed it down as it tumbled through a narrow ravine. Careful not to twist her ankle, she had stumbled through dark woods until, joined by various rivulets, the brook grew into a stream and then finally spilled into the river.

Twice more, a proud explorer, Manda had entered the Hole and secretly visited the river. Neither Papa nor Mama, nor even Thomas, knew that she had. No one would ever think to look for them in the Hole. Hannah would be safe there, Manda thought, if only she could get her inside in time. Manda tore frantically at the brush, trying to move it aside, her fingers cut and bleeding from all the brambles.

The dog and the horses were awfully noisy, awfully close! Manda could tell that they were at the house. Had Hannah's mother and father and Girl made it safely back into the closet? They must be worried sick about where Hannah was. What would Papa think when he saw that she and Hannah were missing? What would he tell Charlie if he noticed that Manda was gone? Would they search for her? Would they then find Hannah? Oh, she'd made a mess of everything, Manda thought, continuing to work at the brush.

At last the Hole was revealed. Crouching and gesturing to Hannah to do the same, Manda gently pushed her in, then crawled in behind. Reaching out, she pulled the pile of brush back into place. The Hole had disappeared again from sight.

Except for the tiny circle of light at the distant end of the tunnel, all was darkness. She and Hannah would sit together in that darkness, Manda tried to reassure herself, listening and waiting until it was quiet and safe to come out again. "We're safe here," Manda whispered to Hannah, hoping that what she was saying was true. "No one can see us, so no one will find us."

"Don't no one need to *see* us," Hannah reminded Manda in a whisper. "They got a dog. He can *smell* us. Won't take him more than a sniff or two."

Twenty

"They're round here somewhere, hidin' out," a deep and unfamiliar voice insisted. It was close, the voice, probably just up the path from the Sad Place, and it spoke a little the way Hannah and her family did, thick and smooth and slow like molasses, but with none of the sweetness in it. "This bit of brown cloth is the proof."

Crouching in their underground hiding place, Manda felt Hannah startle. Then, ever so slightly, ever so carefully, Hannah began to move. She was searching in her pocket, Manda could tell, for the piece of cloth she had used earlier that day to erase the letters of her name—the *HANNAH* she had written on the floor of Manda's room.

Manda put her mouth up to Hannah's ear and, quieter than she'd ever spoken before, dared to whisper, "Do you have it?"

"No," Hannah hissed back. "Must have dropped it in the meadow."

Manda's heart fell into her feet.

"Sure as I'm born, this cloth is slave cloth!" the unfamiliar voice resumed. "We're bound to catch 'em soon! Me and Whitney sure aren't fixin' to return empty-handed. For one, the money's too good! Mr. Williams is offering to pay us double when we get them back to him.

For two, he's plenty angry. Doesn't like what it says to th'other slaves, them getting away. Wants to get them home again and use them as an example. I can see why. So me and Whitney, we intend to catch them runaways, and know what? I'm thinking we're gonna get 'em today! Right, Whitney?"

"Umm. Hmmm," another strange voice answered.

"Course I'm here to help you," yet another voice said. Manda recognized it as Charlie Meecker's. "Wouldn't be doin' my job if I didn't, would I? But now, I got to tell you, Mr. Beckworth, we here are peaceful folk. Why, I've known John Van Dorn since he was a boy. He's a good man. Doesn't want trouble."

"Trouble," One-Word Jake echoed.

"Aren't I right, John?"

"That's right, Charlie . . . Mr. Beckworth. The last thing I want . . . " Manda's father's words were drowned out by the dog's ferocious barking.

"What is it, Snifter?" the man they were calling Beckworth asked excitedly. "Smell something over in that brushpile? Say, Whitney, I think she's found something!"

The dog began to paw at the brush, growling low and steadily, starting to dig his way in. Manda and Hannah huddled together, trying not to breathe.

"Mr. Beckworth!" Papa's voice rang high and nervous above the menacing sound of the growling. "This here is sacred ground. My babies are buried nearby. I can't have your dog messing up this place I carefully cleared to honor my babies that passed. I have to ask you to stop this minute!"

"Good dog! Got something there?" the man called

Beckworth shouted, ignoring Papa's plea. "Keep at it!"

The dog was getting closer. Already he had pulled some of the brambles of the brushpile away, and now a ray of sunlight slit, like a knife, into Manda and Hannah's hiding place. In a matter of minutes the growling dog would make its way through. What should Manda do? Should she try to sneak Hannah down the tunnel to the opening and out into the ravine at the other end? The slightest movement would give them away. Manda couldn't think. She couldn't move. Her mind, and her body, were paralyzed with fear.

Then, all of a sudden, the dog ceased his growling, ceased his digging, and began to bark repeatedly with excitement. What was happening? Had they been detected through the space in the brambles? Now . . . everything was silent. Only the sound of Hannah's frightened breathing and, out beyond the brushpile, the squawk of frightened birds.

"Why, what did you go and do that for?" one of the voices called out angrily. "Are you clumsy, or just plain stupid?"

"Take it easy, Beckworth," Manda heard Charlie Meecker say. "It was an accident. Didn't mean to drop it. Seems like it fell out of my pocket. Always carry a bit of jerky with me, 'n case I get hungry. Your dog, Snifter, diggin' away at that brushpile as if it were a bone, guess he was hungry. Forgotten all about that pile of brambles. Sure does go for jerky!"

"Jerky," One-Word Jake repeated.

"Why, I have a mind to . . ." The man called Beckworth stopped.

"Now look," Charlie Meecker said. "You ain't gonna find a family hidden under a pile of brush, are you? You're only gonna find ground. They ain't around here. Too close to people and the house. No slave family'd be foolish enough to hide here."

Inside the Hole, Manda and Hannah listened. Was it possible? Had Charlie Meecker guessed where they were hidden? Was he trying to save them, or had they just gotten lucky?

"What about this cloth?" Beckworth asked angrily. "Where did *it* come from?"

"Oh, they're round here somewhere, I suspect," Charlie said. "But you ain't gonna find them in broad daylight. They got this far north, they must know a thing or two 'bout keepin' out of sight. . . . I got a suggestion."

"What?" the voice asked suspiciously.

"Come back here tonight when it's good and dark. Sometime round midnight when they're apt to be movin' about. You bring your dog, and I'll get some others with theirs. Seems to me Tommy Bartlett's got a hunting dog, and Bill Snodgrass. Tim McCormick's got one, too, though I'm not sure 'bout Tim's sympathies. We'll come back tonight with the dogs and fan out through the woods. We'll find them that way, for sure. Three or four dogs and a mess of men, we'll find them. What do you think, Mr. Beckworth?"

"Hate to say it, but I guess you're right. Them slaves are expert at disappearing during the day. When it's dark, they come out and move around some. With enough dogs, we'll find them . . . s'long as you leave your jerky at home," he added angrily.

"What do you think, John? Hope you won't mind us coming back here later tonight," Charlie Meecker asked. "You know the new law. Got to do my duty. . . . Mr. Beckworth, you and your associate come with me and Jake. We'll get something to eat and gather up the men. We're gonna leave you now, John. Leave you here to tidy up. Put everything back to rights, but remember, John, we'll be back . . . round midnight."

"Midnight," One-Word Jake echoed.

"Midnight," Papa repeated. "I won't forget."

Twenty-one

Manda and Hannah stayed still, listening for the departing sounds of Charlie Meecker, One-Word Jake, the slave catchers, and—most especially—the dog. They did not budge, nor, it seemed, did Papa, until they heard the whinny of the horses and the pleasing sound of them galloping away.

For a long while, all was still. Then, finally, Manda heard Papa's voice. "They're gone," he said, and Manda began pulling at the brushpile while Papa did the same from outside. In a short time, Papa's long, sinewy arms were revealed. Reaching inside the Hole, he lifted Manda, followed by Hannah, up and out into the startling sunlight.

"Hannah!" Papa said, with great emotion. "Are you all right? I would rather they arrested me and carried me off to jail than that they find you or your family and send you back into slavery."

"I am fine," Hannah answered. "But my family . . . are they . . . ?" She was too frightened to finish her question.

"All safe and hidden behind the closet, but oh, so worried about you. *Manda,*" Papa said sternly, and gave Manda a look that, in all Manda's life, she had never seen before, a look that made Manda wonder if Papa could ever love or approve of her again.

"Papa!" Manda cried, and threw herself against him. "Can you ever forgive me?"

"Better to ask Hannah and her family to do so," Papa answered, but hugged her back. "You are a foolish girl who has put us all at risk. I should . . ." Papa stopped speaking and looked deep into Manda's eyes.

Manda looked back up at him, or tried to. She thought about the danger she had put Hannah and her family in, and her eyes brimmed so full of tears that the world and Papa began to blur around the edges.

"I see that you understand what you have done," Papa said.

Manda nodded, and when she did, two tears ran down her cheek. Before Manda could touch them, Hannah's dark brown fingers were there, soft and quick as a butterfly, to brush them away.

"It wasn't only Manda's fault. It was mine, too. I wanted to go outside."

Papa sighed, shook his head, spread out his long arms, and hugged Hannah and Manda close.

"How did you know where we were?" Manda asked him.

"I didn't," Papa said. "When I heard the horses, I whistled for you. When you did not come, I hid Hannah's family and hurried upstairs to your bedchamber. The window was wide open. You weren't there. The tree . . ." Papa shook his head again at Manda. "It's a good thing your Mama's so quick-thinking. She found Thomas some rock candy she'd been saving for a special occasion and stuck it in his mouth. She told him she'd take it away from him if he said even a single word to anyone. That kept him quiet while I went outside to meet Charlie and his men.

"The dog led us to the brushpile. As soon as he did, I knew you were there, hidden inside. It was Charlie and his jerky that saved you."

"Charlie Meecker," Manda said, wondering. "Did he drop his . . . ? Did he do it on purpose? Whose side is he on?"

Papa shook his head. "I thought I knew, but maybe I don't. Perhaps Charlie has a bigger heart than he lets on. Whatever his reasons, he has given us some time, but we haven't long. He and Jake will be back tonight with those slave catchers, the men, *and* their dogs."

Papa looked at Hannah. "By then, you and your family must be safely on your way. I had hoped to keep you here for another day or two to give you time to rest up before you continued on your journey, but now we have no choice." Papa looked up at the sun. "We must return immediately to the house. Your mama and papa are terribly worried, and midnight will come, sooner than we think. We have much to do before then. As for you, my Manda, this time you *must* obey me. Hannah's future—and her family's—depends on it. Do you promise to do what I say . . . and *only* what I say?"

"I promise," Manda said, and she meant it.

Twenty-two

Hannah was back in the closet again with her family. Papa had said they could not afford to take chances now. He could not be certain that Charlie Meecker could hold off the slave catchers if they decided to return before midnight, nor even whether Charlie would be willing to try. But Papa had determined that the door to the closet could be kept open, along with the door in the closet wall. It would take but a minute to close everything up, if need be.

So Manda sat in a chair in the hall by the closet reading out loud *Two Years Before the Mast,* a book Uncle Oliver had recently given her. She could at least send Hannah and her family the gift of language and the pictures it created, as they waited in their hiding place.

"Can you hear me?" Manda called out to the closet.

"Yes!" "Real fine!" the closet answered.

"'In a short time,'" Manda continued, "'every one was in motion, the sails loosed, the yards braced, and we began to heave up the anchor, which was our last hold upon Yankee land.'"

Thomas sat at Manda's feet, playing with his rolling horses and listening as the salty words washed over him, while Mama clattered in the kitchen fixing food for

Hannah and her family. Some of it was to eat now, and some to take with them on their journey.

Papa had rushed away on his horse, carrying the jam Mama and Manda had put up, saying he intended to deliver some of it to a neighbor or two, but Manda knew better. He was probably carrying it as an excuse, in case someone stopped him on the road. He could tell anyone who asked that he was only taking jam to a sick neighbor, when he was really . . . well, *what* was he really doing? It was all part of the plan, Manda guessed, to smuggle Hannah and her family away tonight. But how? Manda didn't know, and she knew well enough not to ask. Papa would never tell her. She would only anger him, and she'd done more than enough of that for now!

"'Throughout the night it stormed violently—rain, hail, snow, and sleet beating upon the vessel—the wind continued ahead, and the sea running high.'" Manda read, and each moment passed quickly as Manda imagined herself aboard the *Pilgrim.* Afternoon soon slipped into evening, and Manda lit a candle to help her see. She read faster, knowing that the light was fading and very little time remained.

"Manda," Mama interrupted softly. "It's growing nigh unto evening. I'm afraid I have to ask you to stop reading. I need your help. . . . Isaac, Ellen," Mama called out to the closet. "I want to get some supper in your bellies before you have to . . ." Mama's voice caught in her throat. She couldn't continue. It seemed that Manda hadn't been the only one who had made a friend that day!

"Amelia, let me come out and give you a hand," Hannah's mother called out to Mama.

"Yes, please, let us come out and help you," Hannah's father said.

"How I wish it!" Mama answered with emotion. "I'm afraid it just isn't wise. I've cooked honeyed ham, mashed turnips, and cornbread. Manda will pass it to you. How I hate to think of you up there in that dark, dusty place when you should be sitting proper out here!"

"Amelia," Hannah's mother said in her soothing voice, "your cooking's gonna taste as good in a closet as it does at your table. I know, 'cause we here can smell it. My goodness, Girl is gurgling so, I may even give her a taste of your turnips. Now quit your worrying 'bout us, we're fine as beetles in a bottle full o' leaves."

Mama couldn't help but laugh. She brushed a stray ringlet off her face. "If you say so, Ellen," she said. "Come, Manda, I'll serve. You carry."

Like a ferry on the river, Manda came and went, carrying plate after plate to the closet, reaching up as Hannah's hands reached down to receive them. Last, she carried a large bottle of cider and some glasses. "Here, Hannah," she called. Hannah's pretty face appeared at the opening, framed like a portrait. "Hannah," Manda said, needing to say her name, but not knowing why.

"Manda," Hannah said in return.

"Hannah," Manda said again.

"Yes?"

Manda didn't know what she intended to say. She opened her mouth and a few words fell out. "We didn't have enough time. . . . We didn't have time for . . ." Now it was Manda who couldn't continue. She wasn't sure just what she was trying to say, but she was crying now. They hadn't had time for . . . for what? For, well, so *many* things! Talks and walks and . . . giggles and gossip and . . . long days of doing everything and nothing together.

"We *didn't,*" Hannah agreed, and Manda knew that even without her words, Hannah had understood exactly what she was trying to say. "Maybe, one day," Hannah said very softly, "we will."

"How I wish it!" Manda exclaimed. "How I—"

Mama's voice interrupted. "Bring this plate to Thomas and take this other one yourself, Manda."

Manda did, and then she sat down in the chair by the closet to eat. The long, exciting day had made her hungry, and she gobbled down her food like one of Papa's pigs.

And then Papa was back. Manda knew, because she heard him singing, loud. She guessed he was singing so they wouldn't be worried by the sound of his horse. Manda peeked out the window. In the growing shadows, she could just make out Papa, carrying a pair of boots and the jam. Manda had been right. It had only been an excuse.

Papa opened the door, sniffed the food-flavored air, and smiled. He seemed pleased. "Isaac," he called out quietly. "I have boots for you. Seem like your size. Ellen! No need to worry anymore. The train will be leaving shortly, with all its passengers aboard."

"Train," Thomas repeated. *"Ch-ch-ch-ch. Ch-ch-ch-ch."*

"That's right, Thomas, they are going riding on one of the shining new trains."

"We thank you again, John," Hannah's father called out.

"No need," Papa responded. "But to get safely aboard, we must do everything just right. Manda, it's nearly dark now. I want you to take Thomas upstairs and put him to bed. I know it's early. Nevertheless, you are to say good-night to everyone and go to bed, too. Mama and I will finish up down here. No complaints," he said, looking stern again.

"But Papa," Manda protested. "I'm not tired and I want to . . . I need more time to—"

"Manda," Papa interrupted, his voice deeper, darker. "You promised me."

"Yes, Papa," Manda said, softly, "I did. But will I see them again, Papa? Will I?"

"No," Papa said, drawing his breath in and touching Manda's arm to offer her comfort. "I'm sorry to say you won't, so you should say your good-night *and* your good-bye both at the same time."

"Papa?" Manda pleaded.

"John?" Mama asked.

"No," Papa said, in his most serious voice. "Say good-bye, Manda, and go to bed, now!"

"Good night," Manda called out sadly to the closet. She refused to say good-bye.

Twenty-three

Manda glanced over at Thomas, safely tucked away in his small bed. Manda had sung him his favorite lullaby and had rubbed the top of his curly head over and over again, a motion that never failed to send him swiftly off to sleep.

And now Manda sat at the edge of her own bed in her dark room listening for sounds in the house. She wanted so badly to know what was going on downstairs, but she understood why Papa had excluded her and had been so abrupt about sending her to bed. He didn't trust her. Why should he? There wasn't *anything* Papa had told Manda to do that she'd done as he'd asked!

But how could she allow Hannah to leave without having the chance to say a proper good-bye? And so Manda sat at the edge of her bed, wearing her night-clothes over her day clothes, listening. Papa had a plan to smuggle Hannah and her family out of the house to freedom, and Manda intended to discover what that plan was.

While she had been putting Thomas to bed, she'd heard the comforting clank of Mama in the kitchen, putting supper things away. She'd listened to the quiet mumble of voices, too, and the soft rumble of people moving about, but now, though Manda strained her ears to detect the slightest sound, all was strangely silent. Charlie Meecker had said that he and the slave catchers would return sometime around midnight, and although that was still hours away, it was full darkness now and getting later, minute by minute. Manda couldn't stand waiting any longer. She had to know what was happening . . . now!

Removing her boots, she grabbed Coey Yocks and padded to the door of the bedchamber to listen. She could just make out a soft, whispering sound and something that sounded like a hiss.

Moving ever so carefully, Manda crept halfway down the stairs, then paused to listen. Not terribly far away, somewhere near the foot of the stairs, probably just outside the kitchen, her parents were talking, whispering back and forth in excitement. Manda leaned her ear in their direction.

"Hassssssn't come! Sssssomething mussssssst have happened."

Placing her feet at the far edge of each step to keep it from creaking, Manda tiptoed down three steps and then carefully sat down.

"Ssssshould have been here by now. Sssssomething's gone wrong. Sssssomething must have kept him."

Manda dared to lower her body down one more step. Now she could hear perfectly.

"If Jonah doesn't come soon," Mama was saying, "*I* could take your place. Then *you* could lead them, instead of Jonah."

"Amelia!" Papa scolded.

"John, I'm as capable as anyone!"

"Yes, I know, Amelia, but it's far too dangerous. I could never forgive myself if . . . And besides, the two of us alone, we can't do it. We need three people—one to lead, one to keep watch from behind, and *you* to stay at the house, in case they come knocking. You have to be here to keep them awhile . . . pretend they've awakened you while the children and I are in bed sound asleep. Offer them tea. Ask them questions. Keep them as long as you can until we've— *Where* is he?" Papa whispered in frustration. "We need him. He's the only other person besides me who knows the tunnel."

The tunnel! So *that* was the plan, Manda thought. Jonah, who lived down the road, was going to help Papa smuggle Hannah and her family through the Hole and down to the river. No wonder Papa had told Manda never to go there. It was an escape route. No wonder Papa kept it covered over with brush so no one could see it! Manda was filled with determination. Jonah wasn't coming. Papa needed someone to take Jonah's place. Someone who knew the tunnel.

Without thinking, Manda jumped to her feet and called out, "*I* know the tunnel!" and as she did . . . she tripped. Tumbling down the few remaining steps, she landed, with Coey Yocks, right side up, at Papa's feet!

"Manda!" Papa exclaimed.

"Manda!" Mama echoed, hurrying to help her. "Are you all right?"

Manda merely nodded, too startled to speak, too frightened about how Papa would react to her unwanted, unexpected, and quite unladylike appearance.

"I should have known!" Papa said, shaking his head.

"What am I to do with such an impetuous, disobedient daughter?"

"Only listen to me, Papa," Manda pleaded. "I won't cause trouble this time. I only wish to help. You keep watch from behind, as you planned. Let *me* lead Hannah and her family through the tunnel. I can do it!"

"You? Alone? Impossible! It's dark. You're only a child. And you don't know the way," Papa said.

"Oh, Papa, I confess. I know the way through the tunnel into the ravine, and all the way down to the river. I discovered the Hole long ago and have been through the tunnel many a time. I tell you, I know it by heart."

"You may not lead them, Manda. I cannot allow it. Tell her, Amelia!"

"You may not . . . " Mama began, but she didn't finish her sentence. She was thinking, hard. "John?"

"What is it, Amelia?"

"We can't be certain that Charlie can hold off those terrible men till midnight, or even if he means to. They could return any minute. We must act quickly. The three of us together . . . well, maybe we don't need Jonah after all. Perhaps we should let Manda lead them."

"Amelia!" Papa nearly shouted.

"They won't harm her, John, you needn't worry, for just as you said, she's a child. Besides, they're not after *her*. If they appear, you will be following close by, but hidden, keeping watch. I in my nightclothes will stay back at the house in case they come here. We haven't much time, John. Ellen and Isaac are ready now and waiting. Manda says she knows the way. I think she can do it."

Papa's face looked as gray and as troubled as a storm

sky, and Manda felt suddenly frightened at what she had, without thinking, offered to do. It was true she had been through the tunnel many times, but never before at night. If Papa agreed . . . well, then she would be responsible for more than just herself. She'd be responsible for an entire family—Hannah's family. She had to do things right. Could she?

"I hardly know what to think, Amelia," Papa was saying. "I . . . I must be crazy even to consider this, but . . . it seems I have no choice. All right, Amelia. We'll do it. We'll let Amanda lead them."

Manda drew in her breath. "Papa," she said, looking deep into his eyes. "Thank you for allowing me to help. I promise . . . you can trust me. I won't disappoint you."

Papa's body stiffened. "Don't *ever* thank me for putting you and your mother at risk!"

"Don't you worry, Papa." Manda pulled off her nightclothes to reveal her frock. "The three of us together, we'll do it," she said.

Twenty-four

And so only a short while later, Manda, with a hug from Mama, set out across the meadow, without a candle, without a lantern, without a moon to light the way. Hannah and her family followed, single file, carrying a small sack of Mama's good cooking and Girl.

Farther behind, at a distance, Manda knew there was Papa, hidden from sight. At least she hoped there was Papa, for when she turned, she could not see him.

Across the cold, dark meadow Manda walked, listening with fear for the sound of dogs and the humans who owned them, aware of the crunch of every leaf and the hoot of every owl. With one hand, Manda held on tightly to Coey Yocks and with the other extended behind her, she held on to Hannah.

Hannah's mother, wrapped in a shawl Mama had knitted, had given Girl a few of the amber-colored drops back at the house to make certain that she did not cry out. And now Girl slept peacefully in Princess Ellen's strong arms, unaware of any possible danger.

Even in the darkness, Ellen appeared tall and proud, as did Hannah and her father. Before long, the procession arrived at the Sad Place, and then, at the Hole. Quickly, silently, Manda began lifting the brushpile and moving it to one side as she had done several hours earlier.

"You'll need to crouch inside," she whispered to Hannah's parents when she had finished, "especially you, Mr. Williams." And though it was dark, Manda could see Hannah's father's shy smile in response. "Hannah and I will follow," she assured them. "We know what to do."

Hannah's father nodded, then crawled into the Hole and held out his arms to Ellen, who passed Girl to him and then ducked inside. Next, Hannah crawled in, and last of all, Manda, who took one long look into the darkness, searching the shadows for Papa. Was he there, keeping watch? Though she couldn't see him, Manda felt certain that he was. No time to wonder. She and Hannah had work to do. Together they reached outside and moved the brushpile back in place to re-cover the Hole.

Hannah's parents waited while Manda and Hannah completed their task, packing the brambly brush so tight that not a speck of outdoor light could show through. Inside the Hole-that-was-really-a-tunnel it was completely dark now. The small circle of daylight Manda normally saw whenever she secretly visited the Hole was not visible at the other end. It was night now, and so dark that whether she opened or closed her eyes, it made no difference. Manda shivered. Taking Hannah's hand again, she squeezed past Mr. and Mrs. Williams and resumed her lead, with Hannah close behind.

Feeling her way and holding hands in a human chain, Manda, followed by Hannah, then Ellen carrying Girl, and finally Isaac, crept along the inside of the tunnel. Molelike in her movements, inhaling the damp closeness of underground earth, Manda listened for the reassuring sounds of the others' breath and the soft scraping of feet against the earth.

Unable to see, Manda's leading hand suddenly smashed up against the cold, damp wall of the tunnel. Something smooth and wet and wiggly crawled across her fingers. Manda froze in terror and shook the crawly thing away. She was so frightened she could not take another step. Why had she convinced Mama and Papa that she could do this? Manda wished she could be someplace else, anyplace else but in this dark, dank tunnel.

Pretend you are back in the meadow, she told herself. Pretend you are a ship again, carrying precious carg— No! Manda stopped her imagination. This was not a time to daydream. This was a time to pay attention and keep her mind on what she was doing. She had a job to do—the most important one of her life. She had to do it right. She had to hold on to her concentration and her courage and be more like . . . Hannah. What was that song Hannah had sung to keep herself going on her journey? Something about holding on. . . . Hold on, Manda told herself, and took one step forward. Hold on, she thought and took another. Keep your hand on the—what?—plow—yes, that was it!—hold on. And Manda's courage, inspired by Hannah's song, returned.

How long did she continue leading Hannah and her family through the tunnel? Minutes? Hours? Manda couldn't be certain. She felt exhausted, but she concentrated on her task, moving ever forward. In the inky darkness time stretched out forever, and yet Manda realized the minutes were passing far too quickly, for at the end of the tunnel she would lose Hannah—probably forever. She knew she shouldn't speak, but suddenly Manda needed to. "Hannah?" she whispered.

"Yes?" Hannah breathed.

"Hannah Canada," Manda said, and the name gave her the energy to keep on.

More time passed and then—was she dreaming? Manda thought she glimpsed some light. Leaning her head a little to one side, she detected a circle of darkness that was lighter than the dark inside the tunnel—a circle of dark speckled with a few stars and striped with thick black lines that Manda guessed were tree branches. They were nearing the end of the tunnel!

Manda strained her ears. Up ahead, she thought she heard men's voices. Her heart began to beat violently. One voice sounded like Papa's. Could she be sure? But whose was the other voice?

At last Manda reached the end of the tunnel and peeked outside. A man stood in the darkness. He was wearing a long coat with a hood pulled low over his eyes. Was he there to arrest them?

"Manda," Papa's comforting voice whispered. "It's all right. You may all come out."

And so, one by one, they crawled out of the tunnel. In the darkness, Manda looked at the face under the hood. She thought she recognized it. Wasn't this the blacksmith who had come up from the South only a year or so before? "Mr. Titus?" Manda whispered.

"Hush!" the man and Papa responded sharply.

Then the man, who spoke exactly as Mr. Titus did, in the slow Southern way of Hannah and her family, whispered something Manda had heard before. "You've heard nothing, nor seen anything."

Manda nodded.

Turning to Hannah and her family, the man continued. "I'm here to lead you down the hill to the river, so John here, and his brave daughter," he added, "can return home quick as they can. A friend is waiting by the shore to take you across in his boat to the other side, then on to your next stop, a packet boat that should, if all be right, take you all the way up the river to the border and on to—"

"Canada!" Hannah whispered with excitement.

"That's right, young miss," the man, who Manda decided was assuredly Mr. Titus, answered. "No time for wastin'. Be quick now with your good-byes."

Manda's stomach drew up tight and hard as a knot. The moment she'd been dreading was finally here. She shook Isaac's hand and kissed Ellen and Girl. Then she turned to Hannah.

"Manda," Hannah said.

"Hurry," Papa whispered. "It's time to go."

In the starlight, Hannah's eyes glistened with tears. "Remember me."

"Oh, Hannah!" Manda said. "How could I ever forget you?" She held Coey Yocks, always there for comfort, to her chest, but this time, even Coey Yocks couldn't comfort her. Manda looked at the doll she had carried with her all these many years. She'd been a friend and constant companion and had helped Manda through happy times as well as sad. She was part of Manda, and Manda had intended to keep her forever. . . .

"Time!" Mr. Titus's voice interrupted in a sharp whisper.

"Hannah," Manda said. "Coey Yocks belongs with you. Take her."

"Manda?" Hannah asked with surprise. "Are you sure?"

"Yes, I'm certain. I can't go with you, but Coey Yocks can. In that way, we can always be together."

"Know what?" Hannah said.

"No. What?" Manda replied.

"I love you, Manda Van Dorn," Hannah said shyly, in the darkness. "I always will."

Those were the last words Manda heard Hannah say, for it was then that Mr. Titus whisked Hannah and her family away.

Twenty-five

On an early October morning nearly one year later, when the autumn leaves trembled in the trees, awaiting their moment to take flight, Mr. Titus came around to the house with a letter for Manda. With eager fingers, Manda opened it to read:

Dear Manda,

I can read.
I can write.
I am free.

Hannah Canada

P.S. F is for friend.

You, Manda, You!

ENDNOTE

Manda and Hannah's story takes place in 1850, only eleven years before the start of the Civil War, when the country was divided over the issue of slavery. At the time, there were an equal number of free and slave states. But then California wanted to become the thirty-first state. If California, whose constitution did not allow slavery, became a state, the free states would outnumber the slave states. Those who wanted slavery to continue feared that slavery might be outlawed in the entire nation. The Southern states began to talk about breaking away from the Northern ones.

Hoping to prevent a "disruption of the Union" and the outbreak of war, Congress passed the Compromise of 1850. In exchange for allowing California to be admitted as a free state, Congress promised to pass a new Fugitive Slave Law that would be strictly enforced. Any runaway slaves who escaped to free states would be forcibly returned to their owners. It was hoped that this compromise would end the bitter debate over slavery, but it did not. Now, African Americans who fled to freedom on the Underground Railroad were in more danger than ever, and were forced to flee to safety in Canada.

People disagreed not only about slavery but also about the role of women. Only two years earlier, Elizabeth Cady Stanton and Lucretia Mott had organized the first-ever women's rights convention in Seneca Falls, New York, where they declared, "We hold these truths to be self-evident: that all men and women are created equal." This idea was so startling and revolutionary that it angered many people. Among the few who agreed with it were some antislavery people and Frederick Douglass. A former slave, Douglass wrote about his life in slavery; he was a newspaper editor and a stationmaster on the Underground Railroad.

The years leading up to the Civil War were years of intense disagreement—disagreement about the kind of nation America should be.